An Alien from Cyberspace

by
Anne Schraff

Perfection Learning Corporation

Logan, Iowa 51546

Cover Illustration: Michael Aspengren

© 2002 by Perfection Learning Corporation,
All rights reserved. No part of this book may be
used or reproduced in any manner whatsoever
without written permission from the publisher.

For information, contact:
Perfection Learning Corporation
1000 North Second Avenue, P.O. Box 500,
Logan, Iowa 51546-0500.
Tel: 1-800-831-4190 • Fax: 1-800-543-2745

PB ISBN-10: 0-7891-5494-3 ISBN-13: 98-0-7891-5494-1
RLB ISBN-10: 0-7569-0250-9 ISBN-13: 978-0-7569-0250-6
perfectionlearning.com
Printed in the U.S.A.
6 7 8 9 10 11 PP 13 12 11 10 09 08

AN ALIEN FROM CYBERSPACE

1 When Joshua Madison was 11 years old, something awesome happened. He was camping in the Pahranagat Mountains with his mom and eight-year-old sister, Jessica. One night he was searching the sky to find the Big Dipper. His grandfather had shown him how to find several constellations, so he was taking advantage of the clear sky to try his skill.

Suddenly, a terrible bright light appeared. Joshua had never before seen anything so glaring. A glowing oval-shaped object with antennae protruding from the sides seemed to float directly overhead, transforming night into day. It went up, down, and sideways at will.

"Mom! Jess!" Joshua shouted. "Come quick!"

Joshua's mom had come running from the camper. "What is it—" she started to ask when she saw the light. Jessica was right behind her. "Wow, that's so weird," his mom gasped. Jessica covered her eyes with her hands.

Then, as quickly as it had appeared, the thing rose and vanished.

"Maybe it's a UFO," Joshua had said. He hadn't known much about UFOs and things like that, but once he had seen a movie about them.

"Yeah," his mom said lightheartedly, "maybe aliens are landing." She had tried to make a joke of it.

"Mommy," Jessica had whimpered, frightened by the whole thing. His mom put her arm around her daughter and said, "It's nothing, sweetheart. Just ball lightning, that's all."

But it wasn't ball lightning. Joshua knew that. It was something that couldn't be explained. And because of it, Joshua got interested in UFOs and extraterrestrial life. He started reading books and magazines on the subject. He listened to a guy on the radio who talked about nothing but unexplained events, mostly on the high desert where Joshua lived. Joshua became absorbed by it.

Now, at 17, Joshua loved to surf the

AN ALIEN FROM CYBERSPACE

Web, always looking for new information on his favorite subject.

Joshua corresponded via email with several people who shared his passion. One guy, who called himself Orson, believed in alien abductions. He forwarded Joshua chilling messages from people claiming to have been taken aboard spaceships by weird aliens. Orson claimed he was even taken on an alien craft once himself. Joshua didn't know if he believed any of that, of course, but it was fun discussing it.

Then there was Silver Girl. She said she was a teenager like Joshua, and she was collecting serious documentation to prove the existence of UFOs. She was the one who had told Joshua that 26 astronauts with NASA had reported seeing UFOs.

Joshua rarely shared his hobby with fellow students at Truman High. When he did, they just made fun of him. They were into music, clothes, cars, and dating. They used their computers to enter chat rooms and play stupid role-playing games. At least to Joshua they were stupid. He didn't want to pretend he was fighting some green dragon or trying to find a magic potion from a sorcerer.

Joshua's mother had remarried the year before, and Joshua's new stepfather, whom he called Sam, thought the whole idea of life on other planets was absurd. One time when Joshua made the mistake of sharing his thoughts on the subject with Sam, his stepfather had put him down so completely that Joshua vowed never to mention the subject again in his presence.

"Only loonies and wackos believe in little green men with bug eyes landing in flying saucers. The whole idea is ludicrous," Sam scoffed.

On this day, Joshua came home from school as usual, did some homework, then went online. He checked in with his email friends—Orson, Silver Girl, and half a dozen others. If his friends were online, their names popped up on his screen as soon as he opened his email program. Then they could chat through instant messaging about anything new they had come across.

AN ALIEN FROM CYBERSPACE 5

Today Joshua chatted with a highway patrolman who said he had chased a metallic oval for six miles down a lonely desert highway. Then the thing turned on him, and an amazing creature with silvery skin popped from the oval. The patrolman said he took off fast.

No more of his friends were online at the moment, so Joshua logged off. He was getting hungry and knew that his mom would have supper ready soon.

***

About 8:00 Joshua returned to his computer. He was expecting a message from his grandfather on the high desert. He was Joshua's favorite relative. He was computer literate, and he and Joshua emailed each other almost every day. It was cheaper and more convenient than calling. So when Joshua saw that he had mail, he figured it was something from his grandpa.

But the email was not what he had expected.

I am a prisoner of a vicious earthoid. I need help to return to my home. I was taken from my pod by force. Help me please, the message read.

Joshua smiled. The message had come from Orson. Joshua recognized his address at the top of the window on the screen. Orson was a strange guy. He was no doubt playing mind games on his computer, seeing how Joshua would react to a phony plea from an extraterrestrial.

Joshua didn't know Orson that well. He claimed he was a college student, but he and Joshua had never actually talked or met. It was strictly a cyberspace friendship. Orson told Joshua once that he loved everything about Orson Welles, the great old actor. He had many of his movies and the tapes of his terrifying radio program that was broadcast ages ago, the one where he pretended to be announcing an invasion from Mars.

Now, apparently, Orson wanted to mess with Joshua's mind. He must be bored with emailing me those alien abduction tales, Joshua thought. They were sounding more and more far-fetched anyway.

A message popped up on Joshua's

AN ALIEN FROM CYBERSPACE

screen telling him that Orson was now online. Joshua decided to see what he was up to.

Hey, Orson. What's going on? Joshua typed.

Nothing over here, Josh, Orson replied.

Joshua was puzzled. If Orson wanted to pretend he was an imprisoned alien, why was he avoiding the subject? Why didn't he carry on the charade?

Or was the email really from Orson? Was somebody else using his computer? Maybe some kid . . .

Maybe, Joshua thought nervously, the message was a cry for help from somebody in the house. What if there were something dark going on in Orson's place? Maybe a woman or a kid had used the computer to send a cryptic cry for help, and Orson didn't know anything about it.

Maybe, Joshua thought, Orson was some nasty guy who was abusing his family, and the only way they could reach out for help was by sending that strange email just to attract someone's attention . . .

Hey, Orson, we've known each other for a year now, Joshua typed. *Why don't we exchange names and real addresses? It would be fun to get together sometime and discuss the paranormal in person.*

No way, man, Orson typed his reply. *It's email or no mail. Gotta go now, Josh. See ya in cyberspace.*

Joshua shrugged and logged off. He figured it was probably nothing but Orson acting stupid. Maybe he was tired of spinning all those wild tales of being abducted by aliens, so he decided to play out a fantasy where he was the one doing the abducting.

"What are you doing, Josh?" Jessica asked from the doorway. She was 13, but she looked 16. She was tall and athletic, a great volleyball player.

"Just emailing some friends," Joshua said.

"How come that's all you ever do?" Jessica asked. "My friend Lisa has a sister in your class. She says she likes you, but you just ignore her. You won't even talk to her."

"Who is it?" Joshua asked, barely interested.

"Becky Stone," Jessica replied. "She says you're in your own little world. I'm getting tired of trying to explain to Lisa what a weird brother I've got."

"Becky Stone doesn't like me," Joshua said. "She's part of the beautiful crowd."

"Oh, Josh!" Jessica groaned. "How can you spend all your time talking to stupid space geeks on the computer?"

Joshua sighed. "Some of them are very interesting," he tried to explain. "A lot more interesting than the losers at Truman. I don't like sports. So shoot me. I should be going crazy over the basketball team being in the championship, but I couldn't care less. Okay?"

"All you want to do is talk about aliens!" Jessica continued. "Sometimes I think you're not even my real brother. Maybe some aliens came and took my real brother away, and now they're occupying your body." She waved her fingers behind her head like antennae. "Beep, beep, beep!"

Joshua laughed dryly. "Ah, Jessica, you're right. You've got it all figured out. Now why don't you go play with your Barbies or something."

Jessica stormed out of his room, and Joshua returned to the computer. He sent an email to Silver Girl. She had told Joshua her real name—Rina LeClair. She said she was a senior like him. But she had not yet sent a picture. Joshua was really curious about her looks. He was sure she was beautiful.

Hi, Silver Girl, Joshua typed. *Hey, I think Orson's gone off the deep end. I got a message from somebody on his computer claiming to be a kidnapped extraterrestrial asking for help. I've got a hunch it's from Orson himself.*

Silver Girl wasn't online, so Joshua closed out his email and typed an essay for his government class.

He was supposed to be analyzing the advantages and disadvantages of a major third party candidate in a presidential election. With the recent popularity of such political figures as Ross Perot, Pat Buchanan, and Jesse Ventura, Joshua's teacher had been fascinated with debating the effectiveness of a third party, such as the Reform Party. However, Joshua just couldn't seem to stay focused on the pros

AN ALIEN FROM CYBERSPACE

and cons of splitting the American vote three ways. Distressed aliens kept popping up in his mind.

After a half hour, he saved the few paragraphs of his essay he had managed to scrape together. Then he opened up his email again. A message instantly popped up telling him that Silver Girl had come online.

Hi, Josh, Silver Girl typed. *That Orson is a sicko. Maybe there is a poor little extraterrestrial trapped in his lair. Who's to say it couldn't happen? I mean, we always thought one would land . . .*

Come on, Joshua typed. *You're messing with my head now. Orson is just playing games.* Then, changing the subject, he wrote, *Hey, Silver Girl, send me a picture. I want to know if you're as gorgeous as I imagine.*

I'll think about it, she typed. *But you'll be disappointed.*

Let's see, I bet you're about 5 foot 5, with dark hair, dark eyes, and a smile that could attract beings from all over the universe, Josh typed.

Well, sorta, Silver Girl typed. *Gotta run now.*

Joshua grinned and was getting up from his computer when his stepfather appeared in the doorway.

"You on that computer again, Josh?" Sam asked, frowning. "Do you ever do anything but sit at that computer emailing strangers?"

Sam Benedict sounded irritated. Joshua didn't like his stepfather very much. He was a tax auditor for the government. He was pretty sure that most taxpayers were trying to cheat the government, and he did his level best to trip them up.

Sometimes Joshua thought his stepfather didn't leave his sleuthing at the office. He also pried far too much into his stepson's life.

"I'm working on my government homework," Joshua said.

Sam came, uninvited, into Joshua's room. "I'll believe that when I see it." He looked at the computer screen. "So, where is it?"

Joshua felt anger boiling up inside him like lava in an erupting volcano. Sam had that effect on him.

"Look, I'm an okay student," Josh said.

"You're not getting any calls from my teachers, right? I don't have to show you my work. I'll give it to Mr. Spencer in class tomorrow."

"Ha," Sam snorted triumphantly. "You haven't been doing any government homework. You've been spending the whole afternoon and night emailing a bunch of freaks."

"I don't email freaks," Joshua snapped. "I'm interested in space exploration, and so are a lot of other interesting people. Sometimes I talk to physicists and astronauts."

Joshua didn't mean to use such an angry voice with his stepfather. He really wanted to get along with the guy for his mom's sake. But it was real easy to fly off the handle when it came to Sam. He struck Joshua as an unremitting control master.

Joshua wanted to know how Sam got off moving into his house last year and acting like he was his father. That's what really burned him.

"All right," Sam said, "I've had it. You've got no right to use that tone of voice with me, boy. I deserve some respect. No more emailing on school days, understand?"

"You can't give me orders like that," Joshua cried furiously. "You're not my father. You're *nothing* to me. I got that computer from my real father, and you've got no say over when and how I use it. My mom tells me what to do around here—not you!"

Sam marched down the hall. Joshua flopped down on his bed. He knew Sam was going to his mother for her support. Whenever Joshua talked back to the guy, he went running to his new wife demanding that she back him up when he tried to discipline her kids. Jessica had accepted him. She even liked him. But Joshua wanted no part of Sam Benedict as his father.

Joshua hated how Sam always dragged his mother into these situations. Joshua didn't want to make his mother's life harder. After Joshua's father left, when Joshua was about seven, it had been really hard for her. His dad didn't send support money for the first two years. He didn't have a job, and he was drifting around the country like a hobo. His mom struggled a lot. She had had to raise two kids on her own.

Finally, his dad started sending money. So it was getting easier. And now she had Sam. Joshua didn't blame her for finding someone else.

But he didn't want the guy lording it over him either. Joshua figured he had gotten along without a father now for ten years. Now, at 17, he didn't want or need a father figure. Besides, if he needed one, he had his grandpa.

2

Twenty minutes later, Joshua's mom came to his room with the familiar sad look on her face. "Josh, do you have to be so rude to Sam? Can't you try a little harder to be polite, at least?"

Joshua sat up on his bed, where he had been reading an astronomy magazine.

"I'm sorry, Mom," he said. "But Sam treats me like a little kid. He watches me like a hawk, like *I'm* trying to defraud the government or something. He's got no right coming in here and demanding to look over my homework. I mean, what's that about? It'd be different if I were flunking, but I'm doing okay. Anyway, if there's something wrong with what I'm doing, then you tell me. I don't need some guy I scarcely know stomping into my life and taking over."

Joshua's mom stepped into the room and closed the door slightly. "Honey, Sam doesn't mean any harm," she defended.

"He's really trying to help. He's worried that you spend so much time on that computer. I'm worried too. Josh, you used to play basketball, and you had a social life. But now it's just that computer sucking up every spare minute."

Joshua said, "I lost interest in basketball. Anyway, I'm learning a lot on the computer. The Internet has opened up a whole new world. It's exciting, Mom."

"Well, Josh, just try to spend a little less time on the computer, and . . . please, try a bit harder to be nice to Sam," his mom pleaded.

"I'll try," he said.

***

In the morning, Joshua, ignoring the directive from his stepfather, checked his email. He got a message from his grandpa telling him about how his restoration of an old 1948 Chevy was coming along.

But that wasn't his only message . . . There was another strange email from Orson's computer.

Please, please help, the message read. *I may not have access to this computer for much longer. He will discover what I am doing. He will destroy me. I must get home. Please, help me.*

Joshua glanced at the clock. He didn't want to be late for school, but he had to talk to somebody about this. Silver Girl's name had popped up on the screen when he had logged on, indicating that she was online too. She had told him to keep her posted on the strange email he'd gotten. So Josh decided to chat with her real quick.

Hey, Silver Girl, I got another distress call from Orson's computer, Joshua typed. *The message sounded real frantic.*

That's so weird, Silver Girl typed back instantly. *You know what, Josh? I think I know where Orson lives. He was peddling fake moon rocks from his Web site last year. I saw his address when I checked out the site. He lives about 50 miles from you, in a little town called Blue Hill.*

Orson just wants to play mind games with me, don't you think? I mean, how could there really be an alien with access to his computer? Joshua asked.

AN ALIEN FROM CYBERSPACE 19

Unless one crashed near him on the high desert, and he overpowered it and took it to his place, answered Silver Girl. *It could happen, Josh. We both know they're out there, right? One of these days they'll make contact, and then everybody will know. But until then, they're probably doing surveillance. If some demented person like Orson got ahold of one, then it would be a real disaster.*

Joshua was *pretty* sure there were such things as UFOs. After all, a respected physicist from the University of Arizona had said UFOs were real—probably extraterrestrials sent to watch the earth. That happened years ago, and the physicist got in a lot of trouble with his colleagues for the statements. But still, he must have had good reasons to go out on a limb like that.

But Joshua wasn't *totally* convinced. He definitely wasn't as sure as Silver Girl that there really were extraterrestrials roaming the earth.

Silver Girl, what am I supposed to do? Joshua typed. *I gotta go to school now, and there may really be a creature calling for help.*

Josh, Silver Girl answered, *just go on to school. But keep on this. We'll see what happens this afternoon and tonight. If we're sure this Orson guy has some poor alien in his clutches, then we've got to figure out a plan to help it.*

Joshua shut down his computer, grabbed his books, and headed for his Honda. His mom had already gone to work, and Jessica had caught the bus to school. But Sam was still sitting at the kitchen table finishing his last cup of coffee before he went downtown to trap tax cheaters.

"So, running late again, huh?" Sam asked in an annoying voice. "Hard to break away from that computer, isn't it? You're really in trouble, Josh. I think you're addicted to the Internet."

"Don't worry about me, Sam," Joshua answered as he went out the door. "Just go on downtown to your office and try to catch those old retired people who forgot to report their bingo winnings from a Saturday night game at church."

As he started his car, Joshua thought he should probably be feeling guilty. Here he was, mouthing off to his stepdad again after his mom had asked him not to.

But his stepfather had asked for it, he reasoned. Why was he always sticking his nose in Joshua's business? Joshua already had a father, although he only came around maybe twice a year. His father was remarried now with a new set of kids. Joshua didn't have much feeling for him either. His father had abandoned his family. He probably had all kinds of reasons that made sense to him at the time, but Joshua still felt angry about it.

At his age, he just couldn't accept any man in his life, except for his grandfather who had always played straight with him. Joshua was almost a man himself, and that's how his grandfather treated him— like a man. So when he had need of an older male relative in his life, he headed up to the mobile home where his grandpa lived. They hung out together, fixing old cars or hiking and fishing in the mountains.

Joshua drove down Main Street to the east edge of town where the high school was located. It was 8:00, and the community was starting to come alive. Joshua saw a handful of retired men sitting in the local coffee shop, probably drinking black coffee and discussing how their investments were faring. A few merchants were unlocking their shops—the drugstore, the grocery store, the real estate office.

Joshua made the right turn onto School Street and pulled into the student parking lot of Truman High. He locked up his Honda and started for the school, a sprawling brick building with outside corridors.

As he approached the school, he noticed Becky Stone standing in front with her little group of friends. Once or twice he had thought of asking her out because she was cute, but he really hated her attitude. She was too pushy and she gossiped. He hated that. She and her little pals hashed over every guy at school, dissecting each one like a frog in biology class.

Joshua walked down the hall to his first class—physical science. He sat down just as Becky walked in. Her seat was just

AN ALIEN FROM CYBERSPACE

across the aisle from his. "Hi, how's it going?" he asked her politely.

"Great," she said. "How about you? Your sister told my sister that you're getting to be a regular recluse, holed up in your room and talking about little green men from Mars."

Joshua smiled. It wasn't worth arguing about. "I don't think they're green. They're probably more grayish," he said.

Becky laughed and turned to her friend who sat behind her. "Do you think they really look like that wrinkled little guy in that old movie, that E. T.? I think he looked like a turtle. He was really ugly. Josh, do you really believe in that kind of sci-fi stuff?" she asked.

"Who knows?" he said. "I'm not like you, Becky. I don't think I have all the answers to life's most complicated issues. I'm still learning. I email university professors in the science field, and some of them believe in the existence of life on other worlds. We humans can be pretty arrogant. We think we know everything, but we don't. We're still struggling with diseases that have haunted people for thousands of years. Maybe someday we'll meet beings from other worlds who'll have some of the answers we've been looking for."

Becky laughed. "Oh, Josh! Even the government says there's no such thing as UFOs. They did this big investigation years ago, and they said it was all untrue. My dad said that all the UFOs were found to be just natural stuff like balloons and weather stuff, and the people who claimed to see all the extraterrestrial junk were either crazy or liars."

"Do you believe everything the government says, Becky?" Joshua asked. "Didn't you ever hear that the government sometimes covers stuff up because they think people can't handle the truth?"

"Oh, listen to you," she laughed. "Now you're talking like those weirdos who go hide in the mountains and say the government is after them in black helicopters!"

A boy to Becky's right joined in the fun. "Yeah, I heard this nut say that all kinds of little spacemen were captured by the government and taken to some secret military base. Roswell, I think. They were studied and stuff, and then they were killed so people wouldn't find out."

The science teacher, Mrs. Whitney, came in right as the bell rang. She was carrying a stack of papers, obviously having spent her time before school at the copy machine.

She was already white-haired, though she was only in her fifties. She was Joshua's favorite teacher at Truman High because she was so enthusiastic, and also because she respected the students. She treated her students with respect—not like a bunch of silly teenagers she was forced to deal with.

"Mrs. Whitney," Becky piped up, "there are no such things as UFOs, right? I mean there couldn't be life on other planets, right? They're too hot or too cold, or they've got no atmosphere or something. Isn't that true?"

Mrs. Whitney looked at Becky and said, "Well, there couldn't be life on the planets in our solar system, not life in the sense of intelligent creatures. There could be small life-forms, bacteria—but not life similar to human life."

Becky turned gleefully to Joshua, "You see?" she cried. "There are no little green people flying around the sky in silver flying saucers!"

"Becky," Mrs. Whitney said, "I didn't quite say that. I made no mention at all of little green men." There was a smile on the teacher's face. "It's true that we've ruled out the possibility of intelligent life on planets in our solar system, but it would be presumptuous to say that there is no intelligent life on places other than Earth. In fact there are a growing number of astronomers, biologists, and chemists who say there might well be life elsewhere. Whether or not they could make contact with us, well, we just don't know. There are vast distances between galaxies. But then advanced physics talks about distorted space time, so maybe one could go four light years in a second. There is so much we don't know."

"But isn't it pretty likely that there will never be aliens landing on Earth?" Becky asked, wanting to hang on to her opinion.

Mrs. Whitney continued to smile. "It seems hard to imagine such a thing, but then, who knows? Remember, just a few decades ago some of the things we now take for granted were beyond imagination," she said.

Joshua was grateful to Mrs. Whitney, as he so often was. It would have been so easy for her to put the whole idea into the realm of the ridiculous. But she knew that Joshua and a couple of other students were really into the subject, and she didn't want to totally reject their ideas.

Joshua tried to concentrate on school the rest of the day. But when he was supposed to be thinking about the political process, British World War I poetry, the function of a carburetor, or sine and cosine, his mind kept drifting back to his email messages.

When he got home from school and checked his mail, Orson's name popped up on the screen. He was online. But when he received an instant message, he was stunned. It wasn't from Orson—it was from the supposed alien. It was online right now!

Please help. He is getting closer. I am doomed if you do not help me, the message read.

Joshua stared at the computer screen, his hands trembling as he typed a reply.

Who are you, and where are you from? Joshua typed.

Joshua's heart almost stopped when the reply came back to him.

I am from a galaxy far away. My ship was on a scientific mission, and my pod crashed in the mountains. I was captured by a cruel earthoid who was drawn to my plight by the flash of light. I am called Kotoo.

Joshua's hands continued to shake. *Is this you, Orson? Is this some huge mind game you're playing?* he asked.

The message that followed said, *The earthoid who holds me captive is called Orson. I am in dire danger from him. He is going to destroy me because he believes I have no value alive. Then he will display my remains and make much money. Please help me. I have read your communications to Orson for many days, and I discerned in them a compassionate heart. Please do not fail me. You are my only chance. He comes now, so I must not speak with you anymore.*

Joshua got up from his computer and lay on his bed. He stared at the ceiling, not sure what to believe. He still thought it was a giant joke from the twisted mind of Orson. He had told Joshua many times about being captured and humiliated by a band of extraterrestrials. He had said he wanted to get vengeance on them if he ever could. This whole thing had to be a fantasy from his wild imagination.

Orson was just some nerdy college guy riding this game as far as he could take it. It had to be a game, Joshua thought. And when Orson pulled him in and got him believing it, Orson would type, *Ha, ha, ha, sucker* on the computer.

But what if it all was real? he wondered. What if some extraterrestrial was actually imprisoned by this Orson guy? His heart raced at the possibility.

There had been many stories of close encounters of the third kind, actual face-to-face meetings with aliens. Joshua knew that most of them were probably not true. Those people who claimed to see strange creatures in silvery jumpsuits with big eyes, spindly arms and legs, and claws for hands were no doubt drunk, disturbed, or just dishonest.

But what about that guy in Brazil, an uneducated farm boy who told a story of being taken aboard a luminous, egg-shaped object and examined by creatures in gray, tight-fitting coveralls and with shining blue eyes? Even though he was repeatedly questioned, the young man never changed his story. There were scars on his chin and some evidence of radiation poisoning from the experience.

What about the guys in Cisco Grove, California, who were accosted by creatures in silvery gray uniforms who had glowing reddish orange eyes and a glow on their chests? The creatures finally fled in a dome-shaped ship.

Maybe none of it was true, or maybe it was all true. People mostly just laughed at such things, but what if they were no laughing matter? What if the government knew more than they were telling the people for fear of panic?

What if Kotoo were real and in mortal danger?

What if a creature from beyond the bounds of Earth had actually crashed and been captured by Orson? There were a lot

AN ALIEN FROM CYBERSPACE

of people out there without any conscience. Maybe Orson was one of them. He would treat the creature like a wild beast, using it for his own purposes.

Joshua wondered what to do. If he called the newspaper or a television station, they would treat it like a joke. It would be the humorous segment of the evening news. If he called the sheriff or the military, they would think he was crazy. They would check to see if there was a full moon out and attribute his story to that.

Joshua didn't have to think long to imagine the response his story would bring from his mom and Sam.

His mom would be frightened. Sam would feel vindicated.

"I told you that computer would drive him crazy," Sam would gloat. "Now look—it's happened."

But Joshua had to talk to somebody—somebody who would not laugh, who would take him seriously.

He quickly went to the computer and prayed Silver Girl would be online when he needed her.

3

Luckily, Silver Girl was there for Joshua. Joshua relayed the story of his emails from the allegedly captured extraterrestrial.

Where do I go from here? Joshua asked. *I feel in my gut that this is the real deal. But maybe it's because I'm gullible—I don't know. I guess the thought that there's a real alien out there needing my help is pretty exciting. I mean, I'd get to see this creature, to actually see it with my own eyes . . . is that incredible or what?*

Try to feel Orson out, Josh, Silver Girl typed. *Chat with the guy and try to make him show his hand. Don't let on that you're getting emails off his computer, of course. If there is some alien in trouble, that would be the end of it.*

The alien, if it is an alien, said his name is Kotoo, Joshua wrote.

Okay. Don't betray Kotoo, Silver Girl responded. *Just play it cool, Josh. Orson might be feeling pretty good now if he has captured an alien. He's probably dying to brag about it, but he can't. Still, he might let something slip.*

Okay, Joshua wrote. Silver Girl wrote that she had to go, so Josh surfed the Web while he waited for Orson to come online. He got involved in a chat room colloquium about the discovery of water on Mars and what that would mean for the search for life on the red planet. After about 30 minutes, Orson's name popped up in the corner of Joshua's screen.

Hey, Orson, Joshua typed, *I was talking to some guy in Idaho, and he said some people in England came in contact with some aliens. This guy said the aliens had grayish skin and just one eye. He said they really looked weird.*

Bunk, Orson wrote back. *That's all science fiction stuff. They've got skin like brown velvet. They sort of look like baby seals, except they've got arms and legs.*

Joshua felt a chill go down his spine. In all the time he had been emailing Orson, he had never talked as authoritatively about extraterrestrials as he was doing now.

Hey, man, Joshua wrote, *how do you know all that? You got to be an expert awful fast.*

Research, Orson replied. *I've been spending 15 hours a day on the computer. I'm talking to people all over the world, man. I'm getting stories from people who never went to the authorities. I'm compiling it all, and now I have a composite of what these little buggers are like.*

Man, Joshua continued, *wouldn't it be awesome to really eyeball one of them? I mean, to really see one in the flesh. What would you do if you came across one?*

There was quite a long pause before Orson typed his reply. *Well, if you were to get one alive, you couldn't let anybody know because they wouldn't let you keep it. The government would come and take it away from you. Then maybe they'd even arrest you if the thing said you'd mistreated it or something. Some civil rights freaks would come along and say you did bad things to it, even if you had to be rough to capture it, you know. And a guy could end up going to jail. They'd want to say the thing had a soul or something, and you had no right to, you know, cage it up. You couldn't make any money on it, because they'd come down on you and take it away.*

So what would you do? Joshua asked nervously. *Man, I sure wish I'd come across one. I'd make friends with it and, you know, learn all I could from it.*

You know, Orson typed, *they know our language right away. They've got this thing in their brains that can translate any language into theirs, and they can talk to you like they've been here all of their lives. But, you know, to get rich on finding one of them, you'd need to take lots of pictures and stuff, just to prove you really had it. But then you'd have to kill it. Like suffocate it or something. You could say it just died on you, and it wouldn't be alive to make accusations against you, see? Then you'd have all the TV guys and the tabloids eating out of your hands.*

Joshua turned numb. Kotoo was right! Orson did mean to destroy the poor creature! Joshua remembered Kotoo's desperate words.

He is going to destroy me because he believes I have no value alive. Then he will display my remains and make much money.

Hey, Orson, it'd be stupid to kill it. I mean, keeping it alive would be your ticket to fame, Joshua typed.

Nah, Orson answered. *You need to keep it going for a while and take some pictures of it in the wild. Like, you know, go up to the mountains, put a chain on its ankles so it can't go far, and let it flop around. Then, when you tell everybody to come see it, and it's dead and all that, you can say you tried to get help, but it just suffocated. Man, a guy could be as rich as those basketball players—maybe even richer. You could milk a story like that all your life. You could be the guy who actually had contact with an extraterrestrial.*

Hey, Orson, a guy could get in trouble if he killed an alien like that, Joshua typed.

Suddenly the tone of Orson's email changed. *Ha, ha, ha. This is a weird conversation we're having, man. You don't know how funny all this is.*

AN ALIEN FROM CYBERSPACE   37

Someday you'll know.

What do you mean, Orson? Joshua asked.

Gotta go, man, Orson typed. *I got places to go and things to do.* With that, he logged off.

Joshua made up his mind. He had to try to find the alien. He really believed there was one now. He decided he would drive to Blue Hill tomorrow. And he'd try to get Silver Girl, or Rina, to go with him.

Joshua saw that Silver Girl was still online. He typed her a message, explaining everything that was said in his conversation with Orson. Then he said, *I'm telling Mom I want to drive up to see my grandfather tomorrow. I'll stop by his mobile home, but then I want to go to Blue Hill and try to find this Orson guy. Will you come with me? It'd mean a lot if we were in on it together.*

Wow, Silver Girl typed back. *You and me meet. So quick. I'm not sure I'm ready for that, Josh.*

Aren't you close to Blue Hill, Rina? Joshua asked. *You told me once you don't live too far away.*

I'm about 30 miles north of you, she typed. *And Blue Hill is another 20 miles northwest. No problem there, but, wow . . .* Silver Girl typed.

Joshua wondered what the problem was. Silver Girl always resisted sending him a picture. Maybe she looked really strange. Maybe she was embarrassed by something in her appearance. Joshua wanted to find a way to reassure her that no matter what she looked like, they were still buddies—they'd always be cyberspace pals.

Hey, Rina, I don't care if you're ten feet tall with orange hair, he typed. *I still want us to do this together because I really feel close to you. Our minds are on the same track, you know?*

Well, I guess, Rina replied.

Hey, Silver Girl, we've got a mission, you and me, Joshua continued. *We have to rescue Kotoo, right? If there's some poor alien being held captive by a lunatic who means to waste the poor little guy, then we've got to do something!*

Okay, okay, Rina typed back. *Take 93 north to White Horse Junction. Turn left*

AN ALIEN FROM CYBERSPACE

when you see Hank's Market, and keep going to the curio shop with the Indian head on the roof. I'm there. I'll be waiting for you around 10:00. Is that good for you?

That's super. Thanks, Joshua typed. He couldn't remember ever being as revved up as he now was. He was going to finally meet Rina tomorrow morning. Then maybe they'd actually come face-to-face with an alien being from another galaxy!

But now he had to convince his mother to let him go.

"Hey, Mom," Joshua said, finding his mother in the living room having a cup of coffee. She was an executive secretary, and she had a lot of stress in her busy office. When she got home from work, she usually spent about 15 minutes drinking coffee and relaxing. "I'd like to drive up and see Grandpa tomorrow. You know, spend some time with him. I'd be home around 7:00 tomorrow evening. Okay?"

Joshua's mom seemed surprised. "Joshua, don't you remember?" she asked. "We were all going out to the lake and do some fishing tomorrow. Sam's been telling me about this great little lake they just stocked, and I thought it would be really nice if we did some family stuff."

"I really need to go see Grandpa," Joshua said. "He's restoring that old Chevrolet, and I can really be a big help to him. I sort of promised him I'd come . . ."

"It's really inconsiderate of you to make plans with your grandfather without clearing it first," his mom snapped.

"I know. I'm sorry, Mom, but . . ." Joshua muttered.

"Well, Sam is going to be really hurt, but if you've promised your grandfather you'll be there, I guess you'll have to go. Sam will be so disappointed," his mom said.

Sam walked in the door just then and caught the last part of the sentence. "Why is Sam going to be so disappointed?" he asked, looking from Joshua to his wife.

"Oh, hi, sweetie," Joshua's mom said to Sam. "Joshua promised his grandpa he'd go up there tomorrow and help him with some project. Now he can't come on our trip to the lake."

"That's ridiculous," Sam growled. "Family trips come first. Joshua can go

AN ALIEN FROM CYBERSPACE

see his grandfather anytime."

Joshua felt the anger rising again. His stepfather really liked to get to him. Why can't the guy just stay out of my life? he thought. Why can't he see that I don't want or need anything from him?

"I need to see my grandfather," Joshua said persistently. "I don't want to go fishing anyway. I hate fishing. Sticking smelly bait on some hook and yanking some poor choking fish out of the water—"

"You go fishing with Grandpa," Joshua's mom reminded him.

That's different, Joshua thought. When you love someone and just want to be with him, you don't mind sharing in activities you're not crazy about.

But to his mom and Sam he said, "Look, if I go on the fishing trip with you guys, nobody is going to have any fun. I'm going to be so miserable, I'll ruin the whole day for everybody else."

"What a bad attitude you've got," Sam said bitterly.

Joshua's mom had that sad look on her face again, and Joshua felt guilty. But he desperately needed to go to Blue Hill tomorrow to see if there really was a creature called Kotoo being held captive. If Joshua did nothing with the information he had and then later learned the creature was found dead, he would never be able to forgive himself. Maybe it was all a hoax, but he had to give it his best shot and find out.

"All right, Joshua," his mom finally said. "Go see your grandfather tomorrow, but the next time we plan a family outing, you are coming along. Will you promise me that?"

"Yeah, sure, Mom," Joshua said.

***

The next morning Joshua rose bright and early. The rest of his family had left in the early morning for the fishing trip, so it was pretty easy for Joshua to roll out of bed. He had been so nervous that he hadn't really slept.

It was a 40-minute drive to White Horse Junction on 93. Then another 30 minutes to Blue Hill. Joshua took binoculars, a camera, some maps, and a cell phone.

Joshua planned the trip to meet up first with Rina. Then they'd drop in on his

AN ALIEN FROM CYBERSPACE 43

grandpa. After that, they'd be off to Blue Hill.

Joshua was almost as excited about meeting Silver Girl in person as he was about seeing Kotoo, if there really was such a creature. He wasn't sure there was a Kotoo, but there really was a Silver Girl.

Maybe . . . or maybe Silver Girl was not at all what he had imagined. Maybe she wasn't a teenaged girl at all. Maybe she was a 60-year-old woman . . . or a 40-year-old man . . . or a 12-year-old kid. All Joshua really knew was that she was great in cyberspace. But then, that's about all Silver Girl knew about Joshua too.

She's probably as excited and nervous as I am, Joshua thought. Maybe she's afraid a 50-year-old guy in a faded baseball cap will get out of the car in front of the curio shop. She probably has 911 programmed on her cell phone, just in case!

They were really total strangers. They had a strange Internet friendship that could blow up like a pierced balloon when they finally *really* met.

Traffic was pleasantly light on the highway. A cool wind was blowing a misty rain across Joshua's windshield. There was a brief shower, then the clouds moved, and bright sunshine peeked through. It was a perfect day for a drive. Joshua figured that he and Silver Girl would take the ten-minute jog west to see his grandpa and eyeball his restored Chevy. Then they'd be off to Blue Hill to search for Orson and Kotoo.

Joshua turned at Hank's Market like Silver Girl had instructed. Then he spotted the curio shop and pulled up in front. He glanced around, wondering if there might be a pretty girl waiting for him, but he saw no one. After parking, he took a deep breath and prepared to meet Silver Girl.

When he entered the shop, Joshua saw a brown-skinned woman about 40 years old behind the counter. She had glossy black hair and large, pretty eyes. Maybe she was Silver Girl, Joshua thought. Maybe Silver Girl was really a lonely woman trying to break the monotony of living in this tiny town by going online with strangers.

"Uh, hi," Joshua said. "I'm, uh . . . looking for Rina."

The brown-skinned woman smiled and said, "She's in back getting some dream

AN ALIEN FROM CYBERSPACE

catchers. She'll be out in a minute."

"What are dream catchers?" Joshua asked.

"Oh, these little feathered circles here," the woman said, reaching for some hanging near the counter. "They are very pretty, and they catch good dreams for you."

Suddenly a girl appeared. She was so beautiful that Joshua sucked in his breath. She had the same brown skin as the older woman, who was probably her mother. They bore a strong resemblance to each other.

All of a sudden Joshua felt very self-conscious. He was just an average-looking guy. Rina was probably disappointed. If this was Silver Girl, she was way ahead of him in looks.

"You must be Josh," the girl said with a bright, warm smile, her bright red lips parting over white teeth. She came from behind the counter then, and Joshua noticed that there was something different about her walk. He had been staring so hard at her lovely face that he hadn't even noticed at first how she moved. She wore capri pants, and from her right pants leg there was a silver prosthesis.

"Let's go," Rina said to Joshua. "I told my mom about you and how we were going to see your grandfather."

Rina's mother smiled. "I was nervous at first. You hear stories about crazy people on the Internet."

"Yeah," Rina interrupted. "Mom has a good friend who does detective work. She had him check you out to make sure you weren't a psychopath. Bet you didn't know you had been investigated."

Joshua smiled nervously.

"A mother can never be too careful," said Rina's mother. "Actually, the detective is from your area and actually knows of your family. But I got a good report on you, Joshua. And now that I've met you, I can tell you're a good boy. I am so glad you two are finally meeting."

"Bye, Mom," Rina said, rolling her eyes a little.

"Bye, Rina," her mother said. "Use the cell phone if you need to get ahold of me."

Joshua and Rina stepped outside and climbed into the Honda. As she was buckling up, Rina said, "I forgot to tell you about my leg. That's where I got the idea for the

Internet name—Silver Girl. When you laugh at stuff like that, it's not such a problem. I hope you're not uncomfortable with it."

"Oh, no," Joshua mumbled.

"I had cancer when I was 11. It was either me or the leg, and I won. I get around just fine," Rina said. "It was hard at first, but now I hardly think about it. Except when I meet new people . . ."

Joshua turned and looked at her. "When you wouldn't send me your picture, I was worried that there really wasn't a girl like you. I don't have a girlfriend at school, because they all think I'm weird or something. I was hoping you'd be, you know, nice because just emailing you makes me feel closer to you than I've ever felt to a girl," he said.

Rina laughed. "I was hoping you'd be nice too, and you are. I was out of school so long when I was sick that my mom and dad turned to homeschooling me. So I don't get to meet a lot of people my age."

Another cloud burst and splashed heavy drops of rain on the windshield, but it didn't dampen the moods of the two friends inside the car.

4

Joshua treasured his grandpa. He always had. Joshua's grandma had died when he was 13. Joshua spent all that summer with his grandfather, helping him get rid of stuff in the big house and get the essentials brought to the mobile home where he now lived. They got even closer that summer.

"Grandpa, this is Rina, a good friend," Joshua said when they reached the mobile home.

His grandpa grinned. "You Paiute, Rina?" he asked.

"Yeah," Rina said.

"Figured either that or Shoshone," Joshua's grandpa said, winking at his grandson.

Joshua told him that they had an important errand to run, but they'd spend time with him on their way back. "I'll have barbecued chicken ready for you guys," his grandpa promised.

When they were back on the highway,

Rina said, "You're really close to your grandfather, aren't you?"

"Yeah. He's the best. I've got a dad who's missing most of the time and a stepfather I *wish* was missing, so having a cool grandfather has saved me," Joshua said.

Joshua and Rina passed the time to Blue Hill sharing stories and tidbits about their lives. Joshua felt as if he and Rina were old friends. He couldn't believe how affable she was.

After a half hour or so, they drove past a sign that said "Welcome to Blue Hill."

Blue Hill was a small town with one main street. Joshua and Rina drove past a grocery store, a hardware store, two video rental places, and a couple of bars and restaurants. They pulled up at the post office.

"When Orson was selling those phony moon rocks on his Web site, his box number was 76," Rina said. "He wanted people to post their credit card numbers so they could do the whole deal online, but if they wanted to send checks, that was the address."

"Maybe he's standing in there right now checking his mail," Joshua said with a wry grin.

"Yeah, right," Rina said.

They went inside the empty post office and spent a few minutes staring at box 76. The post office clerk, of course, gave out no information on box holders.

"I wonder if his real name is Orson," Joshua said as they walked out. "He claimed he used the name in honor of his hero—that actor Orson Welles, but maybe he had it legally changed. He might be that weird."

"So let's just ask around town if anybody knows of a guy named Orson who peddles moon rocks over the Internet," Rina said. "In a tiny place like this, people usually know one another's business."

They first entered the little grocery store. There were old-fashioned dairy cases along one wall and three aisles of various canned and boxed goods. The wooden floors creaked when the two walked toward the counter.

"What can I do for you young folks this

AN ALIEN FROM CYBERSPACE

morning?" a middle-aged lady asked. She looked like just the kind of person who would know everybody in town.

"Uh, we're looking for a guy named Orson who sold moon rocks around here," Joshua said.

The woman laughed heartily. "Moon rocks! Whoever heard of such a thing?"

"It was over the Internet," Rina said.

"Oh, I'm not surprised. You can peddle most anything there. I guess you could offer a two-headed snake and some fool would buy it. I don't bother with that nonsense," the woman said.

"Well, thanks anyway," Rina said as they walked out the door.

Joshua and Rina tried the other small stores on Main Street. Nobody had ever heard of a person named Orson or moon rocks.

Afterwards, Joshua and Rina stood underneath a canopy in front of the hardware store. It was noon, and they stood and looked out over the desert landscape that started just at the edge of town. "Man, we're getting nowhere fast," said Joshua. "This Orson guy must be a total hermit for nobody to have heard of him."

"Wait a minute," Rina said. "He's an Orson Welles fan, right? I bet he goes to the video store and rents old Orson Welles movies."

"Yeah!" Joshua said. "That's a great idea. Come on."

They returned to the video store where the clerk had never heard of a man named Orson who sold moon rocks. "Hey, we're back," Joshua said. "Does anybody ever come in here looking to rent old Orson Welles movies?"

"We're trying to track down this old neighbor of ours," Rina said, "and he was a big Orson Welles fan."

The tired-looking woman behind the counter nodded. "You must mean Mr. Cuttler. You'd think he'd buy some of the movies, but he always rents them. Over and over. He just took *The Third Man* out for about the seventh time. And the funny part of it is, he doesn't even seem to *like* the movies. Couple times I asked him, 'Well, did you enjoy *Citizen Kane*?' and he just growled at me."

"So, where does he live?" Rina asked.

"Oh, you can't miss his house," the woman said. "It's that big old red house at the end of Furnace Creek Road. You just go as far as you can down Roadrunner Lane, and you'll come to this long dirt road. That's Furnace Creek Road. It has a nice view of the Pahranagat Mountains, but that's about all you can say for it."

"Thanks a lot," Joshua said as they left the store. He turned then to Rina. "Boy, are you a genius!" he said. "I never thought of asking about Orson Welles fans!"

It continued to drizzle as they drove down Roadrunner Lane and then turned onto Furnace Creek Road.

"I hope we don't get stuck out here," Rina said. "That sure is a spooky old house in the distance."

"I don't think it's raining hard enough to turn the road to mud," Joshua said.

They pulled up to the old house and parked. A rusty old van was parked out front. It was covered with hostile messages about the government and people in general. "Boy," Rina said, "he's probably a real crackpot."

"Yeah," Joshua said, "the house is just standing out like a sore thumb. Nothing but cactus around it. Like nobody ever planted *anything*."

"Let's tell the guy when he answers the door that we were looking for a copy of *The Third Man* because we're Orson Welles fans too, and we heard he rented one," Rina said.

"Kind of weak," Joshua said. "But I can't think of anything better."

They walked past the old van to the door and knocked. As they waited for someone to answer, Joshua thought that it was hard to believe that the man living in the broken-down old house was the cyber pal with whom he had found so much in common.

He had to knock three times, each time a little harder, before the door finally opened. A man about 75 or 80 years old appeared in the doorway. He supported himself with a cane.

"Yeah? What do you want?" he demanded.

He was about the last person in the world that Joshua expected would be

AN ALIEN FROM CYBERSPACE

Orson, his fellow UFO fan. But he sure looked mean enough to have trapped and imprisoned an extraterrestrial!

"Uh, sorry to bother you, sir, but we were hunting for a copy of *The Third Man*, and we were just wondering if maybe you were finished with your copy. They said in town that you'd rented it, and—" Joshua said.

"I got a week on it yet. I wish those fools would keep their noses out of my business and stop gossiping about me," the old man snarled.

"You're, uh . . . Mr. Cuttler, right?" Joshua asked.

"What if I am? What's it to you?" he snapped.

Joshua decided to push his luck. "I guess you live here alone, huh? Must get lonely . . ."

"None of your confounded business, but since you asked, Sylvestor lives here with me."

"Sylvestor?" Joshua asked, his heart pounding.

"Sylvestor is my shotgun, and if you're not off my property in the next 20 seconds, you'll be hearing from Sylvestor," Mr. Cuttler said.

In a burst of courage that Joshua admired, Rina stepped up and said, "We're really sorry to have bothered you. You have a right to be annoyed. But I just wanted to say that it's great that you're online, using the Internet. A lot of people your age don't get into computers."

The old man blinked in surprise. Then he said, "I don't know what you're babbling about, girl. I don't know anything about those computers. If you ask me, they're the work of demons. I have nothing to do with them." With that he slammed the door.

Joshua and Rina walked back through the light mist to Joshua's car.

"He couldn't be Orson, Rina. He just couldn't be," Joshua said. "The guy I'm emailing is younger. I know he is by the way his messages are written."

Rina turned and glanced back at the red house. "I'd give anything for a peek inside that house," she said.

"Yeah, Rina," Joshua said, "why don't we try to get in? I'm sure Sylvestor would *love* to meet us!"

Joshua and Rina drove back down Furnace Creek Road toward Blue Hill. Before they could leave town, Joshua had to stop for gas. He pulled up to the lone gas station on the edge of town. After filling up, Joshua headed inside. Rina followed him in to buy a couple of sodas.

"You're new around here," the blonde girl at the cash register said. "We don't get many new people through here."

"Yeah, we just stopped by to visit somebody," Rina said.

"This place is like the end of the world," the girl said in disgust. "We don't have gambling like Vegas, and most folks bypass us. But you should've been here a couple weeks ago when we had the big excitement."

"What happened?" Joshua asked.

"Oh, didn't you hear?" she said, becoming animated. "It was on TV and everything. The TV stations around here anyway—maybe not where you live. But two fellas, truck drivers, were coming down the road in their rig, and they got chased by one of those UFOs. It hovered up in the sky, an egg-shaped thing, glowing these terrible blue lights that blinded them."

"So, what happened? Did the thing land?" Joshua asked.

"Well, the guys said it was making this loud buzzing sound," the girl continued. "They were scared out of their wits. It hovered for a while; then it shot straight up and went toward the Pahranagat Mountains."

"Uh, who are the guys who saw all this?" Joshua asked. "Do they live around here?"

"Sure. The Duncan brothers. They have the lumberyard right down the road. Can't miss it. Only one in town," the girl said.

Joshua and Rina thanked the cashier. Then they headed off for the lumberyard. When they pulled into Duncan's Lumber, they found one of the brothers outside. Al Duncan seemed eager to talk about what he described as the most incredible experience of his life. "I was on TV and everything," he boasted. "I was like some big celebrity."

"What exactly happened?" Joshua asked.

AN ALIEN FROM CYBERSPACE

"Well, this thing came at our truck like it meant business," Al described. "Me and Charlie were petrified. But then the thing made this buzzing sound and rose up. The lights, I never saw anything so bright in my life. Was like looking at the sun."

"Then what?" Rina asked, listening acutely.

"Well, we kept on watching the thing," said Al. "Watched her go up and down, sideways, like nothing I ever saw. Charlie either."

The hairs on the back of Joshua's neck stood up. He remembered when he was 11 and the terrible bright light had appeared from the cylindrical object. It was near the Pahranagat Mountains too.

"Well," Al continued, "then it soared over the mountains, and it seemed like it dropped something, like a parachute or something. This thing came down fast, and then there was a kind of a popping sound. That was the last we saw."

"What do you think it was?" Rina asked.

"Well, just between you and me and the fencepost, kids, I figure what we were looking at was one of those UFOs. I think we saw a real, live UFO. I'm telling you straight, me and my brother have caught a lot of teasing and mockery since all this came out. But I'm not changing my story. What we saw was nothing from this world," Al said.

"Do you think it crashed up in the mountains?" Joshua asked.

"Maybe that thing that dropped crashed, but not the big ship," Al replied. "And another thing too. My brother and me, we got out our binoculars, and we looked real hard at this egg-shaped ship—and we saw faces looking from the windows."

"Faces?" Joshua asked, growing a little weak.

"What kind of faces?" Rina asked. She grabbed Joshua's hand.

"Well, I only know one thing. Me and my brother both saw the same thing. But it was the darndest thing we ever saw. The faces . . . they weren't like *human* faces at all, and they weren't these big heads and bug eyes that Hollywood has been dishing out to us in these alien movies either," Al said, shaking his head. "The faces looked like, well—those baby seals I've seen pictures of. Harp seals, I think they call them. I'm telling you, that ship looked like it was full of harp seals."

Joshua went numb.

Orson's email came back to him like a blow.

They sort of look like baby seals, except they've got arms and legs . . .

5

When they returned to the Honda, Joshua's voice throbbed with excitement. "Rina, what the guy said about the aliens looking like baby seals—Orson said the same thing! I think this is real! The alien ship went down over there in the mountains, and Orson, or Mr. Cuttler, whoever he is, captured Kotoo!"

"So what are we going to do?" Rina asked.

"I can't just go visit Grandpa and then go home," Joshua said. "I've got to try to help Kotoo. I sure can't tell Mom and my stepfather that I need to stay here longer so I can rescue an alien! They'd think I was totally crazy. But Grandpa will understand."

Joshua and Rina drove back to his grandpa's home. Joshua's stomach was growling—both because he was nervous and because he was hungry for his grandpa's chicken!

After Rina and Joshua ate, Joshua told his grandfather the whole story of Kotoo.

"Well," his grandpa said, "I'll tell you up

front that I don't really believe in UFOs and aliens and that sort of stuff. We get our share of strange lights out here on the desert, but I've always thought there was a logical explanation for everything. However, I'm willing to keep an open mind."

Joshua convinced his grandpa to call his mom. He figured that storms in the area had probably cut their fishing trip short.

When he got ahold of her, Joshua's grandpa told his mom that Joshua wanted to stay overnight and most of Sunday if that was all right. Joshua's mom wanted to talk to her son then, so he took the phone.

"Hi, Mom," Joshua said. "I'm having such a good time, I was wondering if I could come home late tomorrow instead of today."

"Well," his mom said crossly, "I'm making a nice pot roast tomorrow, and you know how you like that. I was making it mostly for you. But if it means that much to you to stay over for another day, I guess it's all right."

Joshua knew that his mom still had some guilt over the divorce. So she tried to let Joshua see his grandpa as much as he wanted.

"Thanks, Mom," Joshua said. "And there's always enough pot roast left over for sandwiches, so I'll be looking forward to that."

When Joshua hung up, he grinned gratefully at his grandfather. "Grandpa, you're the best!" he said.

But his grandpa wasn't smiling. "Maybe I'm just a foolish old pushover," he said. "I don't feel real comfortable with you kids storming off to search for this alien. If some loony guy has really trapped an extraterrestrial—this Kotoo creature—then we're dealing with a dangerous person. You kids are no match for somebody like that. What's wrong with calling in Sheriff Salmon? He's a good man and a friend of mine."

"No," Joshua argued. "We can't get the law involved. If they went bursting in that house, even if they got Kotoo alive, he'd never get away again. The government would want to keep him under wraps and study him."

"Joshua, you're starting to sound like those wackos who think the government is always the enemy," his grandpa said.

"It's not that, Grandpa, but you know they wouldn't just let Kotoo go," Joshua said. "Besides, if we went to the sheriff with a story like this, he'd just laugh and think we were nuts."

"Can you imagine the sheriff agreeing to search that house for an alien?" Rina asked, siding with Joshua.

Joshua's grandpa fell silent for a few moments. Finally he said, "Okay, if you kids are bound and determined to go snooping around for this alien, I'm going along with you to make sure you don't do anything real stupid. We'll take my pickup."

"Sure, Grandpa," Joshua agreed quickly.

"This guy, Mr. Cuttler, he was bragging about having a shotgun," Rina said.

"Great," Joshua's grandpa said. "So that means we're not going to be trespassing on his property."

Before they left his grandpa's mobile home, Joshua called his sister on her private phone. She was always tying up the family phone, so for Christmas last year she had gotten her own phone line.

"Listen, Jess," Joshua said, "will you go check my computer and see if I got any mail? I'm kind of playing a game with some guy, and we're emailing stuff back and forth. We're pretending this alien is stranded on Earth."

"You're such a freak," Jessica said. "But I'll go look."

When Jessica returned, she said, "You got a lot of junk mail. Nothing from anybody about aliens."

So Kotoo hasn't communicated with me anymore, thought Joshua. That was ominous. Maybe he couldn't.

"Thanks, Jess," Joshua said. "See ya later." He hung up.

At 3:30 that afternoon, the pickup with Joshua, his grandpa, and Rina rolled into Blue Hill. Joshua's grandpa went off in one direction to try to find out some information about Mr. Cuttler. Joshua and Rina went off in another direction, also trying to ferret out information. All three met at 5:00 in the small pizza parlor to pool what they had learned.

"Cuttler has been living in that house for about five years," Joshua's grandpa said. "He's a crusty character. Nobody likes him because he really keeps to himself. Doesn't take kindly to anybody getting close to him. He doesn't seem to know anything about computers. Never talked to anybody about UFOs either."

"Yeah," Rina said, "that's about what we got too. One lady told me Mr. Cuttler has

AN ALIEN FROM CYBERSPACE

really bad eyesight, that he failed his last driving test. So it would be hard for him to use a computer."

"So maybe we're off base," Joshua said. "Maybe he's just an eccentric guy who rents some Orson Welles movies and has nothing to do with this Orson guy who emails me," Joshua said.

Joshua's grandpa washed down a chunk of pizza with root beer, wiped his mouth, and said, "Except I got on the right side of a gal in a coffee shop. I told her she was a dead ringer for Connie Stevens."

"Who's Connie Stevens?" Joshua asked.

"A real pretty actress who was on TV before your time, Josh," his grandpa explained. "Anyway, my inquisitive friend at the coffee shop goes to the post office a lot, and she said she had a box next to one where Mr. Cuttler used to come last year and take out tons of mail. It used to bother her how he'd stand there pulling out mail so she couldn't even get to her box. She got curious why this old man was getting all this mail, and so one time when a letter slipped to the floor and he missed it, she opened it up and peeked inside before she returned it. Turns out there was a check for moon rocks!"

"So Orson *is* Mr. Cuttler!" Joshua cried. "That's amazing. He must be leading some kind of a double life. A grumpy old guy who seems ignorant of computers and is actually emailing around the world about UFOs!"

"It's incredible," Rina agreed. "How would he even know how to set up a Web site?"

The trio left the pizza shop. Joshua needed a computer. He remembered seeing one in the video store earlier. The clerk had said that they make extra money by renting out time slots for the use of the computer and the Internet. They headed back to The Movie House. Joshua rented the computer for 30 minutes. Then he sat down at the PC, accessed his account, and sent an email to Orson.

Hey, Orson, what's up? he typed. *Listen, man, I need to talk to you real soon.*

Joshua didn't have to wait long before he received an answer.

AN ALIEN FROM CYBERSPACE

Hey, Josh, I know what you've been up to, the message read. *I should've known you wouldn't leave well enough alone. I've seen your ugly face, man. Don't rake up that Nevada dust. It's toxic. You get my meaning. Don't email me anymore. You bore me. Watch for me on TV with the 'remains' of the century. Orson.*

Joshua broke into a cold sweat. He turned to Rina and his grandfather. "He knows I'm nosing around the house. Orson is in there all right. Maybe he's already done away with poor Kotoo, but maybe not. We've got to get in that house right now!" Joshua said.

"Josh," his grandpa said, "I'm calling Charlie Salmon. He'll meet us out there. He has the authority to go in and search if there might be someone in danger. That's all we'll tell him. We think someone is being held hostage. That's a good enough reason for the law to go in, but not for us, a trio of freelancing desperadoes. Listen to me, Joshua. You two kids don't have much of a chance of saving that Kotoo, if there is such a creature, but maybe Charlie can pull it off . . ."

6

"Okay, Grandpa," Joshua said. "Call the sheriff."

Rina looked relieved. Joshua understood that she was probably pretty reluctant to take on the old man and his shotgun.

The three piled into Joshua's grandpa's pickup right after he made the phone call to Sheriff Salmon. They headed for Furnace Creek Road and the big red house where Mr. Cuttler lived.

"Charlie doesn't move so fast now that he's put on some weight," his grandpa said, "but he's a good man. He gets things done. Not too much crime around here, thank goodness. I guess because we got a pretty sparse population."

Sheriff Salmon was parked on Roadrunner Lane when the pickup arrived. He got out of his car and asked, "Hey, Jim, what's this all about?"

Joshua's grandpa introduced Joshua and Rina to the sheriff. Then he said, "My grandson here has been having this email friendship with a guy who seems to live over there in that red house. Anyway, some of the emails that Joshua has been getting lately are disturbing. They sound like the fella may have taken somebody hostage. Might be just a fantasy thing the fella has fabricated, but on the outside chance that we're dealing with something real, we'd like you to check it out."

Joshua was grateful to his grandfather that he didn't mention the extraterrestrial angle. Sheriff Salmon looked like a pretty down-to-earth sort of guy. It was pretty improbable that he would believe the story of Kotoo.

"Well, there's been an elderly man, Ambrose Cuttler, living in that house for several years now. I got called out here once when boys were throwing rocks at his house. He was pretty irate. I can't imagine him doing something as bizarre as kidnapping someone," the sheriff said.

"Yeah, it's pretty hard for us to understand too," Joshua said.

Joshua found the sheriff staring right at him now. "So you're telling me that Mr.

Cuttler and you been emailing each other, young fella? That doesn't sound right to me at all. The few times I've talked to him, he won't have a thing to do with modern gadgets. Wouldn't even give up his rotary telephone."

"I don't know what to think," Joshua said. He felt uncomfortable, the way Sheriff Salmon was looking at him with those narrowed, skeptical eyes. "I thought the guy I was talking to in cyberspace was a young guy like me . . . the way he sent messages and all . . ."

"Okey-dokey," Sheriff Salmon said, "we'll just see what's going on. You folks stay put right here. I will go to the door and ask very politely if I can have a look inside the house. If we think there's a real urgent need to get into the house quickly, then we'll send for backup. Otherwise, Deputy Frank and I will handle it."

The sheriff drove his car to the front of the house. Then he and his young deputy stepped out. Joshua, his grandfather, and Rina pulled up then in the pickup.

"Wow," Joshua said, watching the scene, "what if there really is an extraterrestrial imprisoned in that house? Wouldn't that be the most incredible thing that's ever happened?"

"Oh, if there is a Kotoo, I hope he's okay," Rina said. "I couldn't stand it if we were too late."

They watched in silence as the sheriff and his deputy knocked on the front door of the house. They had been only knocking for a few seconds when the door opened.

"Look, he answered," Joshua said.

"I don't think so," Rina said. "The door seemed to be ajar."

They all continued to stare at the house. Paint was peeling off the door in large strips. It was an ill-kept house with warped roof shingles and two broken windows.

"The sheriff is going in," Joshua said.

"He's being real careful," his grandpa said. "Could be that Mr. Cuttler is hiding in there with his shotgun . . . Could be that leaving the door open was a trap. This man could be real sick."

Sheriff Salmon and his deputy had drawn their guns. They moved slowly, by inches, into the house. They disappeared inside and were out of sight for about five tense minutes before they both came out. The men were moving quickly now. Sheriff Salmon went to his car and began talking on the radio. Then he walked toward the pickup where the three waited.

"We're getting the medical examiner," Sheriff Salmon said in an even, controlled voice.

Joshua's heart seemed to stop for an instant. The medical examiner. That was the coroner. There was a dead body in that house. It was just as he had feared. Poor Kotoo was dead. They were too late to save him. The extraterrestrial had made his desperate plea for help, but Joshua didn't get on it fast enough.

Joshua grew angry at himself. Why hadn't he called the law right away when he suspected Kotoo was in danger? Why was he so concerned about appearing crazy? Why did he put what people thought ahead of the safety of a precious life?

"There are signs of a struggle," Sheriff Salmon said, "and a probable weapon

AN ALIEN FROM CYBERSPACE 75

near the body. Blunt force, looks like. The old man was pretty frail. Didn't take much to put him down."

"Mr. Cuttler?" Joshua gasped. "You mean *he's* dead?"

"Yes," Sheriff Salmon said.

"But what about—" Joshua was about to blurt out the whole story, but he stopped himself. It quickly dawned on him that if Mr. Cuttler was dead, maybe Kotoo had killed him. Maybe the poor extraterrestrial had killed the old man in self-defense. In all the stories Joshua had read about close encounters of the third kind, the aliens always seemed small and weak. But maybe that wasn't true in this case. Maybe Kotoo had been able to overpower his captor.

Sheriff Salmon came closer to Joshua. "We did a quick look around. Didn't see anybody else in the house. Now, since we got a dead body, most likely a homicide, I want some more information from you, Joshua. What made you think that Mr. Cuttler had taken somebody hostage?"

"Well, uh . . . like Grandpa said, some guy who called himself Orson and I have been emailing each other for about a year. In the last few emails, he kind of hinted that he had a prisoner. But all the messages were real cryptic. The guy was into the paranormal. I mean, the whole thing could have been role playing," Joshua said.

Joshua was now terribly afraid for Kotoo. If the poor creature had killed his captor in self-defense and fled off into the mountains, he had to be out there somewhere, alone and terrified. He had no food, no friends. Kotoo probably feared the military from this world would come hunting him for killing the earthling. If Kotoo were caught, who would believe an extraterrestrial when a human being had been killed?

Or maybe the sheriff and his deputy had not looked closely enough in that house, Joshua thought. Maybe Kotoo lay dead too. Maybe Orson and Mr. Cuttler were two different people after all, and Orson had killed Mr. Cuttler *and* Kotoo . . .

"Well," Sheriff Salmon said, "we're only starting the investigation. We'll be wanting to talk to you some more, Joshua. Might

AN ALIEN FROM CYBERSPACE

have been that Mr. Cuttler was living in a fantasy world. Lot of magazines about UFOs and space travel lying around. And there's a big computer in the basement. Most likely somebody he met on the Internet came and killed him."

Joshua, his grandpa, and Rina got back into the pickup and headed out.

"Most likely Sheriff Salmon is right on," Joshua's grandpa said. "Mr. Cuttler was a troubled soul. He probably contacted a lot of strangers just like he contacted you, Josh. He was pretending to be a young fellow, and he probably attracted some weirdo with a UFO obsession. The guy just came out and killed him. That story about the extraterrestrial was probably just a fantasy, Josh."

"Terrible thing to have him murdered like that," Rina said, shaking her head.

"It's the world we live in," Joshua's grandpa said. "Some fellas will kill a man for a few bucks. Some drifters might've just come by and got in an argument with the man."

They rode in silence for a few minutes. Then Joshua's grandpa spoke again. "I wonder if Mr. Cuttler had a family. Maybe sons and daughters he's lost touch with. Often happens that way. Later on I think I'll touch base with Charlie about funeral arrangements. If nobody else is around, I'll help bury him. Make sure there's a ceremony, a few flowers. Any man deserves that."

"That's nice, Grandpa," Joshua said.

Joshua didn't know what he believed. He was so convinced now that Kotoo was real—but maybe his grandpa was right and the whole story was just a fantasy in an old man's feverish mind.

They drove Rina home, and then Joshua and his grandfather returned to the mobile home. Joshua couldn't sleep though. He lay on the sofa bed, tossing and turning and worrying about Kotoo. And then, suddenly, Joshua sat up, wide awake. It was 4:00 a.m.

The van was gone! Joshua just now remembered that the rusty van he had seen parked at the red house was gone! The killer must have fled in it. Or maybe Kotoo drove off in it.

Joshua got out of bed and wrote a note

to his grandfather.

> Grandpa,
> I couldn't sleep. I took your truck. I'll be back soon. If you need wheels, use my Honda.
> Love, Joshua

Joshua grabbed his binoculars and cell phone and got into the pickup. He had thought about just calling the sheriff in the morning to tell him about the missing van. But then he decided he had to give finding Kotoo a shot first. Joshua didn't want to unleash the dogs on Kotoo right away.

Joshua could just imagine the sensationalized headline if it turned out that an extraterrestrial had killed Mr. Cuttler.

Monster Alien Slays Elderly Man

The story would be heavily promulgated by the press. The National Guard would probably be called out to hunt Kotoo down. There would be panic in the country. It would be chaos. People would fear that there were other Kotoos lurking around, plotting to kill other citizens. It would be like that crazy Orson Welles radio program where people thought monsters from Mars were attacking New Jersey.

Kotoo wouldn't have a chance. They might even corner him and shoot him down like a wild animal. That's what they'd think he was too, especially if he had fur and a seal face!

Joshua was tense when he reached the red house in the dawn darkness. Yellow police tape surrounded the place. But he didn't plan on going near the house. He wanted to examine the tire tracks where the van had been parked. Recent rains had made the earth soft enough to yield some clues.

Joshua shone his flashlight on the ground and saw that fresh tire tracks led to a dirt road that seemed to wind its way into the Pahranagat Mountains. Joshua quickly decided to follow the tracks. He had to try to find Kotoo before anybody else did.

AN ALIEN FROM CYBERSPACE

Joshua had to give the extraterrestrial a fighting chance to find a friend and give his side of what happened in the red house . . .

7

The sun was coming up as Joshua traveled the sinuous dirt road. He planned to follow it as far as it took him, stopping at intervals and looking into the distance. He didn't want to drive into a dangerous situation. Maybe Kotoo had the shotgun and would now see Joshua as another adversary.

Joshua scanned the area with his binoculars, making a wide arc of the cliffs ahead. Then something caught his eye—a flash of white against a reddish earthen cliff. It was the white van. It looked like it was parked on the shoulder of the road about a mile ahead.

Whoever had killed Mr. Cuttler was probably close to the van, Joshua reasoned.

He looked at the cell phone in the cab of the truck. He knew he should call Sheriff Salmon right now and tell him he'd spotted the van taken from Mr. Cuttler's yard. In just a short time, this mountain would be swarming with the law.

AN ALIEN FROM CYBERSPACE

And if Kotoo was near that van, he would see the throng of humans closing in on him in great numbers. Then he would probably blast at them with the shotgun and would die in a hail of law enforcement bullets. Who would blame Sheriff Salmon and his men for killing a murderous extraterrestrial?

Joshua decided that he couldn't call the sheriff. Not right away. Not until he tried to contact Kotoo and convince him that he did, indeed, have a friend in this world.

Joshua pulled the pickup off the road into the brush. Then he continued toward the van on foot, moving silently and unseen through the thicket. He planned to take Kotoo by surprise. They had emailed each other. Surely he could convince the alien that he was a friend.

Joshua stopped from time to time to peer through his binoculars. The back doors of the van were open. As Joshua drew closer, he smelled coffee brewing. Kotoo drinking coffee? That didn't sound right. But who knows? he thought.

Then, suddenly, when Joshua was only about 50 yards from the van, he heard a twig snap behind him. He spun around, his heart pounding. And there, in the brush, he saw the most amazing sight he had seen in all his 17 years.

The creature was about 5 feet 2 inches tall and slender. It wore a black leather vest and black leather shorts. Its arms and legs were covered with a fine, golden brown, velvety fur. Its face and hands were smooth, like a human's skin, except for a light peach fuzz. The eyes were large compared to the small nose and mouth. The face came forward a bit, and yes, it looked like a baby seal's face. The creature was obviously an adult, but there was a sweet youthfulness in its features. There was a strange, wild beauty that touched Joshua's heart.

"I am Kotoo," the creature said in a soft voice.

And Joshua knew for sure that Kotoo was a girl.

He never expected the creature would be a girl.

The large, dark eyes widened then and filled with terror. Kotoo immediately crouched down in the brush, and Joshua realized what was frightening her. There was

AN ALIEN FROM CYBERSPACE

a man over by the van, and he was cursing a blue streak.

"Stupid alien!" he screamed. "Where did you go now?"

Joshua saw it then—a chain linking Kotoo's ankles, hobbling her step. Her captor had made sure she could only move short distances, making escape impossible, especially in this rough terrain. Joshua knew that you needed to make long steps when you climbed over boulders.

"You show yourself, or you're in big trouble when I find you!" the man shouted. Joshua could tell he had been drinking. His speech was slurred. That was probably what had made him careless in watching his captive.

Joshua rushed to Kotoo, picking her up. She was light, especially for him. At 6 foot 2, he weighed 175 muscled pounds. He and his grandfather often camped in these mountains, and Joshua had found a few caves. They were excellent hiding places, especially in the spring when the shrubbery covered the entrances. He searched in his memory for the nearest cave.

Joshua figured they could hide until dark, and then they could hurry down the road to the pickup.

Joshua scrambled over a small ravine and spotted the nearest cave. Just as he had remembered, the entrance was obscured from the casual observer. He had to plow through the shrubs with Kotoo to get in.

"You all right?" Joshua asked Kotoo when he put her down.

"Yes," she said. He remembered Orson telling him that aliens had something in their brains that allowed them to translate new languages and speak them perfectly. Orson had pretended it was something he had learned on the Internet, but he must have discovered it through Kotoo.

"Are we safe here?" Kotoo asked.

"I hope so," Joshua said. "I'm Joshua. You emailed me on the computer."

"I know," said Kotoo. "I am so glad you found me. You must be very clever. When I saw you, I knew you must be him."

"Kotoo, tell me what happened in that house," Joshua said.

"The man, Orson, kept me there, in the

AN ALIEN FROM CYBERSPACE

lowest room. You call it the basement. He had his computer there. He also had a cage. He said monkeys were kept in the cage, but the monkeys died. So he locked me there. I could see him emailing several others. I could read the messages even from the cage. I discovered compassion in your words, so I chose to contact you. I could write my messages to you using only my thoughts and my eyes. I could make the keyboard do my will, but the earthoid, Orson, did not know this. I waited until he was out of the room to contact you. He told me he would study me and then destroy me. Then he would be rewarded for finding my remains," Kotoo said.

"How did Orson get you?" Joshua asked.

"I am a scientist," Kotoo explained. "Our ship hovered in your atmosphere collecting chemicals that are needed in our world to make medicines. I was lowered in a pod to gather samples of the air, but my pod crashed. I was not hurt because it came down slowly, but there was a flash of light that drew Orson. He overpowered me and took me to the red house."

"What about the older man?" Joshua asked.

"Orson said the house belonged to his grandfather," replied the alien. "He said his grandfather could not walk on stairs, so he would never discover me in the basement. But the old earthoid did come down, and he found me. He was angry. He said he was calling the law, and Orson picked up the stick the old man used and hit him on the head. Then the life force left the old man. And then Orson said he must now surely kill me because I witnessed this terrible thing."

Joshua stared at the girl. "Where are you from, Kotoo?"

"You asked me that before, on the computer. I am from another galaxy. My sun is brighter even than yours. My night sky has more stars. My world is very beautiful, and I long to go home," Kotoo said forlornly.

"How would you be able to get back?" Joshua asked.

"If you would take me to the pod that crashed, I could call the mother ship to hover above me. Then the force of the light beam would draw me into the ship, and I would be on my way home again," she said.

"Well, don't worry, we'll get you there," Joshua promised, though he was far from sure himself. Orson was roaming around out there, too close for comfort. And he had a shotgun. Plus, Joshua had foolishly left his cell phone in the cab of the pickup.

"You are so very kind," Kotoo said.

Joshua smiled at her. "Is everyone in your world like you? I mean the fur . . ." he said.

"Oh, yes, we all have fur," she said. "When I first saw earthoids, I thought the clothing they wore was their fur. But you have no fur at all except on the top of your head. That is so very strange."

"Shhh!" Joshua said, hearing noises outside the cave. Orson! Maybe he had sobered up enough to find this place and he was now out there with his shotgun. Joshua knew that Orson wasn't worrying anymore about the remains of an alien making him rich and famous. He would be killing a witness to a murder now.

8

"Is he here?" Kotoo gasped in a faint whisper.

Joshua put his fingers to his lips and said, "Shh!"

The twigs outside the cave crackled as something large moved about, but if it was Orson, he did not speak.

Kotoo sniffed the air and smiled. "It is not him," she said.

"You sure?" Joshua asked.

"Yes. We have excellent senses of smell. It is what you call a sheep that makes the noise," she said.

Joshua peered through the brush outside the cave to see a bighorn sheep scampering off.

Kotoo curled up and sat still. Joshua figured that was her way of resting. Joshua closed his eyes and dozed off. He didn't know what to do except relax and wait for it to get dark.

After a few hours, he got up and once again examined the chain binding Kotoo's

AN ALIEN FROM CYBERSPACE

ankles. He wanted to break it so when they made a run for the pickup, he wouldn't have to carry her all that distance.

"I wish I had my grandfather's toolbox," Joshua said. "It's down in the pickup. I think I'll try to sneak down and get it. I'll grab the cell phone too, and call for help if I can."

Kotoo looked frightened at the prospect of being left alone.

"I'll run both ways," Joshua promised. He cautiously stepped outside the cave and then moved down the trail as fast as he could.

Joshua considered himself lucky when he made it swiftly down the trail, crawling from the rocks a few yards from the pickup. Now he just had to grab what he needed and get back to Kotoo.

But, as Joshua emerged from the brush, a sharp voice crackled in the air. "I knew you'd come back to the truck, sucker!" Orson said, aiming his shotgun at Joshua.

Joshua stared at the young man with the reddish beard. He had hard, mean eyes. "You Orson?" he asked.

"Yeah. And you're that nerdy little

Joshua, right? I saw you spying on me at the house," Orson said. "Most likely she's told you everything by now."

Joshua thought fast. He tried to look perplexed. "Who's *she*?"

"Don't play stupid with me," Orson said. "She got in touch with you on the computer, and somehow you found her. Now you've got her hidden somewhere."

"I wish I knew what you were talking about," Joshua said.

Orson looked confused. Joshua could tell that he wasn't sure now what to believe. "You've been snooping around here, right?" he asked.

"Yeah, sure. You hinted that you saw this extraterrestrial, and I got curious. Tell me, Orson, is there really some alien wandering around here?" Joshua asked. "When I saw your van missing, I came on up here. Is it around here, the alien, I mean?"

"You leveling with me?" Orson asked.

"Yeah, sure, man," Joshua said. "I just want to see an extraterrestrial," Joshua said.

Orson's beady little eyes glittered. The

AN ALIEN FROM CYBERSPACE

shotgun in his hand wavered, and then he lowered it. "Okay, listen up," he said. "I captured one of those extraterrestrials, all right. It's a female. But it got away. We gotta find it. We gotta join forces and find it, Josh. It's real smart, but it's dangerous too. It can look at you in a certain way and make you sick. I chained its ankles together so it can't get far, but somehow it sneaked off. We can share the money we'll get from this big story."

"Sounds good," Joshua said, trying to remain poised so Orson wouldn't catch on.

"Listen, man, I haven't told you the half of it. I was living in that red house with my grandfather. I took that alien in, and then it killed my grandfather. Beat him to death. But it's so clever, it's going to say I killed the old man if the law gets it alive. So we can't let the thing live. It's not human. It's no more than a muskrat. So when we find it, we have to, you know, put it down," Orson said. "Then we'll say we found the remains, and we'll make plenty of money off that."

"Yeah," Joshua said, his mouth so dry he thought he'd choke.

"I took some pictures of the thing.

They're in the camera in the van. Those pictures will sell for a fortune, Joshua. We'll split it right down the middle. But first we got to find it. So, how about if we fan out. Do you know this country?" Orson asked.

"Yeah," Joshua said. "You go to the east of this road and I'll go to the west. We'll meet back at the van in an hour. One of us will have found it by then."

"All right. Listen, this is going to be so big. We'll be rich and famous," Orson said.

Joshua went to the pickup and took out his grandfather's toolbox. Then he looked for the cell phone.

It was gone. Joshua figured that Orson must have taken it when he first arrived at the pickup, before he made an ally out of Joshua. He didn't know of a way to get it back now without arousing Orson's suspicion.

He had directed Orson to search for Kotoo in the direction opposite the cave where she waited. Now Joshua ran back toward the cave, the toolbox in hand. He figured he could cut Kotoo loose and they would both be back at the pickup while

Orson was still wandering around the eastern half of the wilderness.

Kotoo was curled up with her head down when Joshua returned. She looked scared and vulnerable.

"I've got pliers and a saw," Joshua said as he ran into the cave. "I'll have you free in a few minutes."

Joshua knelt by Kotoo's feet and worked with the pliers. He couldn't get any of the links wider. So he sawed through one of them and made a deep groove. Finally, using the pliers again, he broke the link. Kotoo's ankles were free.

"Come on," Joshua said, "we're taking off right now. I ran into Orson, and I convinced him I didn't know anything about you. Right now he's on a wild-goose chase looking for you. By the time he realizes he's been duped, we'll be down the mountain."

They scrambled from the cave and started running down the trail toward the pickup.

When they reached the truck, Kotoo climbed into the cab. "Will you take me to the mountain where the pod is so I can call my people?" she asked.

"Yes. I won't ask you to hang around this world, Kotoo," said Joshua. "I'm not saying bad things *would* happen to you, but they could. If I were you, stranded on a strange planet, I'd want to go home too."

Joshua got in beside Kotoo and turned the key to start the engine. It didn't make a sound.

"Oh, man," Joshua groaned, jumping from the cab. He yanked open the hood. The battery had been ripped out. Orson must have done that when he found the truck, thought Joshua. He probably wanted to make sure he and Kotoo, if she was with him, could not escape.

"Ohhh," Kotoo groaned. "Now what will we do?"

Joshua noticed the battery smashed against a rock a few feet away. It was beyond repair. "I don't know. I'd hate to have to walk ten miles down this mountain . . ."

"Joshua, this battery . . . is there such a battery in the van that the earthoid Orson owns at his camp?" Kotoo asked.

Joshua grinned. "Kotoo, you're brilliant!

AN ALIEN FROM CYBERSPACE

We'll go get his battery and put it in the truck!"

The pair hurried up the one-mile trail to Orson's camp. As they walked, Joshua said, "I sure wish it'd been me instead of the creep Orson who found you. I would've liked to introduce you to everything on Earth. I would've loved to ask you so many questions about your world."

"I wish this also," Kotoo said.

They moved quickly toward the rusty van directly ahead.

"Can you take the battery thing from that van and put it in the truck?" Kotoo asked.

"I think so," answered Joshua. "My grandpa taught me a lot about fixing engines." He often helped his grandfather change oil and repair radiators.

Joshua opened the hood and started unhooking the battery cables. Within a few minutes he had the battery free. "Here we go," he said, lifting the heavy battery from the van's engine.

Joshua was breathing hard from all the exertion, and he almost missed seeing the camera on the front seat of the van—the camera that was full of pictures of Kotoo. Joshua grabbed it and took it along, strapped to his shoulder.

When they reached the pickup, Joshua quickly hooked up the battery cables. He rushed to the cab and tried the ignition. The engine turned over with a growl.

"Let's roll!" Joshua shouted.

They started down the mountain, but they got only about a mile when the figure appeared in the road ahead. Orson was standing there, shotgun in hand.

"Stop, or I'll blow your heads off!" he screamed.

Joshua pushed Kotoo's head down. "We're not stopping!" he yelled, stepping on the gas.

As the pickup hurtled past Orson, he fired the shotgun. Joshua lowered his own head as much as he could without losing control of the truck. Another shotgun blast blew out a rear tire. Joshua hung onto the steering wheel on the twisting mountain road.

A sheer cliff alongside the road yawned dangerously as the truck veered. The truck was bouncing violently, and twice they almost went plunging over the side. They were riding on the tire rim because the rubber was torn from the steel by gunfire.

"We've gotta keep moving," Joshua cried. "If we stop, we're both dead!"

9

Screeching and smoking, the pickup roared into Blue Hill. Joshua jumped from the cab and placed a call at the gas station to Sheriff Salmon.

"This is Joshua Madison," he said. "Mr. Cuttler was killed by his grandson. He's up in the Pahranagat Mountains by the Rattler Turnoff. He's got his white van up there, but it's not going anywhere 'cause it lost its battery. He's got a shotgun, and he's dangerous."

"Okay," Sheriff Salmon said, "I need to talk to you, Joshua. Where are you?"

"I'll get in touch with you as soon as I can," Joshua said. "I gotta get something else done first." He didn't want to disclose any more information to the sheriff just yet.

Joshua looked around. He knew the pickup wouldn't make it any farther. The tire and rim were shot. He spotted a four-wheel drive Jeep parked by the mechanics' garage, which had already closed for the day. He ran up and looked inside. Sure enough, the keys were in it. The mechanics probably left it here for the owners to pick up, Joshua thought. I can borrow it and hopefully return it before they know it's missing. He didn't feel he had any other choice. So he and Kotoo jumped inside and took off.

They climbed a mountain according to Kotoo's directions. It was just a pair of tire tracks in some places, but eventually she found her pod. She ran to the twisted piece of machinery and soon let out a shriek of joy. "I think they heard me! I think my contact pulse is still strong enough. I think they are coming for me, Joshua!"

He stared at the willowy girl with both awe and sadness. He thought that she was beautiful in her own unique way. He would have loved to ask her so many questions and tell her about his world. He would have treasured spending time with her. But all that was impossible. It was futile to think about it.

"They are coming, but it will take a little time," Kotoo explained.

"I wish it would have happened differently. I wish I would have had the chance to know you better," Joshua said.

"I wish, too, that my visit to your world had not been so sad," Kotoo said. "I am sorry I met the worst in your world. But I am glad I met you because now I have met the best too."

Joshua smiled. "When I was a boy I thought I saw a UFO hovering around here. I've always wondered if we were being visited from space. I've dreamed how wonderful it would be to actually meet a being from another world," he said.

Kotoo reached out and grasped Joshua's hands. Her hands were soft and warm. The tops of her hands were covered with velvety golden brown fur, but the palms were smooth.

"Joshua, for many years we have been taking chemicals from Earth's atmosphere to use in the production of medicine," she said. "We need the medicine to treat a disease that afflicts many people in our world. We must continue to get these chemicals. Please do not tell anyone about me so that cruel men from your world ferociously search for us and make it impossible for us to get what we need."

"Okay," Joshua promised. "But when the sheriff catches Orson, he'll spill the whole story about you, and then they'll know..."

"But you must not support his story," Kotoo pleaded. "If you say you never saw me, then the sheriff will think Orson's story is just another wild tale. He will think Orson made up the story to explain the death of his grandfather." Suddenly then, Kotoo's eyes widened, and she looked stricken. "The photographs. He had a camera, and he took many pictures of me. Ohhh, the sheriff will find them, and then everyone will know about us . . . we shall be exploited!"

"No, no," Joshua said, "I have the camera. When I took the battery from the van, I grabbed it too."

Kotoo seized Joshua in a strong hug. "You are so wonderful, Joshua. You think of everything! You must destroy the photographs of me. If they fall into the hands of your television reporters, then we shall never be able to return to the Earth's atmosphere for the chemicals we need so desperately!" Kotoo said.

"I will," Joshua promised. But in his heart, he did not know if he would destroy those precious photographs or not. The idea that he had in his possession actual pictures of a being from another galaxy was so awesome. It was the most incredible thing that had ever happened to him. He knew it would be really hard to destroy the pictures.

The sky was almost dark now, but suddenly it began to grow light. Joshua thought for a moment that it was lightning from a mountain storm. Recently there had been thunderstorms in the area.

But it wasn't lightning. It was Kotoo's ship returning.

Kotoo looked up. "Oh! I am going home. I am really going home! I had almost lost hope! I thought I would never again see the faces of my mother and father . . . and the tender face of Oxla . . ."

"Oxla?" Joshua repeated.

Kotoo's face took on an expression Joshua recognized from the faces of girls

AN ALIEN FROM CYBERSPACE

on Earth. The shy smile. The self-conscious tilt of the head. The look of a girl in love. "Oxla is my dear one," she said.

Joshua felt a wild mixture of emotions as the ship lowered in the sky, shedding radiance in all directions. It looked like the glowing oval Joshua had seen when he was 11. He was awestruck and excited but also deeply regretful that it was all coming to an end. He was witnessing something few people were ever privileged enough to see.

Kotoo turned to Joshua a final time. "Thank you for my life. Thank you for allowing me to go home," she said.

"Good-bye, Kotoo," Joshua said. He had a lump in his throat.

Kotoo suddenly wrapped her arms around him, and Joshua bent down to kiss the soft, pink lips. Her lips were warm and tender, like the lips of any girl.

Then the pod from the mother ship lowered. The light became too bright for Joshua. He covered his eyes to protect them from the terrible white light.

When Joshua opened his eyes again, Kotoo was gone. She had entered the pod and had been drawn into the opening bay of the large ship that hovered in the sky. Joshua was alone on the hill. The floating, glowing object was rising so quickly it would be out of sight in seconds.

Joshua watched the ship until it was like a distant star, and then even that vanished. He turned and walked back to the Jeep.

He raced back into Blue Hill and to the gas station where he had borrowed the Jeep. Luckily, no one seemed to notice it had been missing. Joshua nonchalantly returned the Jeep to where it had been before. Then he went inside the station and bought a new rim and tire for his grandfather's truck. He drove out to his grandfather's mobile home.

When Joshua arrived at the mobile home, he found Sheriff Salmon, his grandfather, Rina, and her mother.

"You gave us all quite a scare," his grandpa said as Joshua parked the truck and walked up the driveway.

Joshua hugged his grandfather, and then he hugged Rina.

"Joshua, we need to talk," Sheriff

Salmon said. "My boys rounded up Orson. He admitted he was Mr. Cuttler's grandson, but he denied he killed the old fella. He's telling a preposterous story about some wild extraterrestrial who came into the house and killed his grandpa. I need to check some things out with you."

Joshua called his mother and told her he would be home in a few hours. Then he sat down with Sheriff Salmon.

10

"Joshua," Sheriff Salmon said, "you told me that you and this fella, Orson, were emailing, and you figured from what he was saying that somebody was being held prisoner in that big old house. He's telling us that he told you about this extraterrestrial creature who was in the house, the one he's saying killed his grandfather. What do you know about that?"

"Well, I was emailing back and forth with Orson, and we often talked about UFOs and stuff like that . . . I guess he did say something about an alien landing in the mountains, but he said a lot of crazy stuff, and I never believed him about the alien. He was saying there was somebody in his house who didn't want to be there though, so I figured he'd kidnapped somebody. That's when I called you, sheriff," Joshua said.

"You followed his van up into the

Pahranagat Mountains? He claims you went up there after him and saw the alien," Sheriff Salmon said.

"Yeah, I followed the van, but I didn't see any alien up there. Just Orson. He threatened me and said he was going to blame his grandfather's killing on this extraterrestrial, but I never saw any sign of the bug-eyed alien he was talking about," Joshua said.

"He's saying you helped the alien assailant escape from him," the sheriff said.

Joshua smiled at the middle-aged sheriff, "Yeah, right," he said.

"So," Sheriff Salmon said, a grin spreading on his ruddy face, "you didn't see any little green man up in the mountains, right?"

"Right," Joshua said. "I swear to you, I never saw any little green man up in the Pahranagats. I sure would've liked to though. I've always wanted to see one of them."

The sheriff was laughing now. "The little scumbag is saying the extraterrestrial was a girl, a girl with fur on her, like an otter," he said.

"An otter girl!" Joshua roared, slapping his thighs.

"Yeah, and she had a face like a baby seal, he says," Sheriff Salmon chuckled, reveling in the humor of the situation. "Sounded like she was a right sweet little thing."

Joshua laughed again. "I sure hope that when I meet an extraterrestrial, it looks like that!"

"You and me both, boy," Sheriff Salmon said. He turned serious then. "Just one more thing. Orson claims he took a lot of photographs of the alien, and they're in his camera. He said he left the camera in the van, but we didn't find any camera. Did you see one?"

"A camera?" Joshua said. "Can't say as I did..."

"Well, no doubt it's another of his lies," the sheriff said. "No matter. We got him dead to rights. The old fellow was killed with his own cane, and we figure the prints on that cane will cinch the case. I guess that's all, Joshua. You can go home now."

"Thanks," Joshua said.

AN ALIEN FROM CYBERSPACE

"I got your address and phone number in case we need anything else. Let me know if you think of any more pertinent information. But most likely we've got an open-and-shut case here. Orson has a long criminal record. Just got out of prison last year and came to sponge off the grandfather. I guess the poor old guy got tired of it and wanted to give the punk his walking papers, and that was when Mr. Cuttler got the cane walloped over his head," Sheriff Salmon said, shaking his head.

Joshua waved the sheriff off, and then he turned to Rina. Her mom went inside with Joshua's grandfather for a quick cup of coffee before they headed home.

It was evening now, and the desert sky was filled with stars.

"Joshua, what really happened up there in the Pahranagats?" Rina asked.

"Rina, you're the only person I'll be telling this to. You've got to promise never to repeat it to a soul," Joshua said.

"I promise," Rina said.

"Okay, I trust you," he said. He told Rina everything then. He told her about the narrow escapes in the mountains and about sweet, gentle Kotoo and how she escaped in a pod dropped to her from the brilliantly illuminated mother ship.

"Oh, wow," Rina said when he finished. "Oh, wow!"

"Yeah," Joshua said. "Can you imagine what fun it would be to go on the Internet with this story and share it with all the people who've been talking UFOs with me?"

"You'd be a celebrity, Joshua. Magazines and TV people would be all over you. You could make a fortune just giving interviews," Rina said.

"Yeah, but I promised Kotoo I wouldn't tell anybody about her. Her people need to take chemicals from our atmosphere to make a medicine for a disease they have. If it became known that UFOs were really taking chemical samples, Kotoo's people would be scared off forever," Joshua said.

"You really think if it got out, the whole story I mean, that the government wouldn't respect the right of Kotoo's people to take those chemicals they need?" Rina asked.

"I don't know, Rina. I'm afraid that getting to see and capture the extraterrestrial would be the main goal of our government, and a lot of other governments too. They'd say it was a security thing, that the aliens were a danger to our planet. There wouldn't be much support for just letting Kotoo's people keep on taking the chemicals," Joshua said.

"I hate to think that," Rina said.

"Yeah, Rina, but look, we've got a way on this planet now to eradicate all life on Earth. Just think, our ancestors couldn't have wiped out the planet, but we can. We made the weapons that can do it. All the weapons are still sitting around waiting for just the right crisis to push the button . . . Rina, if we maybe someday would be willing to destroy all *human* life, then how much would *they* count, a strange tribe of extraterrestrials who look like harp seals?" Joshua said.

Rina finally nodded. "Yeah. I guess you're right. If you promised to keep her secret, then you have to," she said.

"Yeah," Joshua said.

Rina asked shyly, "Was she pretty?"

"Yeah," Joshua said. "Not at first. She looked really weird at first, but then when I got used to her, she was really pretty."

"It is so awesome what you saw, Joshua," Rina said. "I bet you'll never in all your life forget what happened to you."

"I guess not," Joshua said. "I know the UFOs are real now. I hope maybe someday they land again and it can be peaceful and stuff, you know? Maybe in a few years all the big weapons will finally be destroyed, and the whole planet will be peaceful. Then it'll be safe for Kotoo's people to land in the open."

"I hope so," Rina said. "Then maybe I'll get to see Kotoo and her friends . . ."

Joshua knew Rina's mom would be out any second. Then it would be time for them to leave, and for Joshua to jump in his Honda and head home too.

"Hey, Silver Girl," he said, "we'll still email each other, right?"

Rina smiled. "Sure, if you want to. I didn't think in all the excitement you'd still want to bother with me . . . I'm just an ordinary, run-of-the-mill girl," she said.

"You're no ordinary girl to me. I feel like I've known you for a long time. We've talked so much on the computer that I feel like we're old friends. You know what's weird, Rina? I go to school with a lot of girls, but I don't feel close to any of them. But I feel real close to you," Joshua said.

"I feel the same way, Josh, about you," Rina said.

They leaned toward each other in the darkness, and Joshua kissed Rina with her black, silken hair blowing against his cheek.

***

On the ride home, Joshua thought about the camera in the trunk of his Honda. Maybe, he thought, he would stash the camera with the undeveloped film and wait until the right time to show it. Maybe when the world was more peaceful and people were more tolerant, maybe then the time would be right to show the pictures . . .

Wouldn't it be fantastic, Joshua thought, if one day on this planet all life was so sacred, even extraterrestrial life, that Joshua could reveal his treasure?

But what if before that glorious day, Joshua had an accident and was unconscious and the camera fell into the hands of somebody else?

What if that somebody else would not respect the needs of a distant world to get chemicals for medical use?

What if the pictures were made public, and a frenzy of alien hunting was launched that would destroy Kotoo and her people?

Joshua pulled off the road while he was still miles from home. He went to the trunk of his car and got the camera. He looked up at the millions of stars shining from unexplored galaxies in the wondrous night.

Then he exposed the film.

Joshua drove the rest of the way home then. He felt strangely lighthearted. He was looking forward to seeing Rina again. She was one special girl. He thought he would try to get along better with his stepfather too. Yeah, the guy was a pain in the neck, but he wasn't a horrible person.